Disabled Fables

Aesop's Fables

Retold and illustrated by artists with developmental disabilities

Star Bright Books
New York

Published in the United States of America by Star Bright Books, Inc., New York.
The name Star Bright Books and the Star Bright Books logo are registered trademarks of Star Bright Books, Inc. Please visit www.starbrightbooks.com.

ISBN 1-932065-97-0
Printed in China 9 8 7 6 5 4 3 2 1

Designed by Tina Trent

Library of Congress Cataloging-in-Publication Data

Disabled fables : Aesop's fables / retold and illustrated by artists with developmental disabilities
p. cm.
ISBN 1-932065-97-0
1. People with disabilities, Writings of, American. 2. Developmentally disabled--Fiction. 3. Animals--Fiction. 4. Fables, American. I. L. A. Goal (Social services agency)

PS508.P56D57 2004
700'.87'50973--dc22

2004017154

Table of Contents

Foreword

In January 2001, I was invited to L.A. Goal, an agency on the West Side of Los Angeles. The purpose of my visit was to research the role of a mentally-disabled man for a motion picture called *i am sam*.

When I arrived, I was greeted by L.A. Goal's no-nonsense, passionate Executive Director, Petite Konstantin. This is not a woman who suffers fools like me easily. At her direction, I was thrust into participating in that day's chore: T-shirts emblazoned with the artwork of my fellow workers needed packaging. I was now a part of an assembly line comprised of the developmentally-disabled men and women of L.A. Goal. I had no idea how to pack T-shirts in plastic, but I was surrounded by skilled packers, generous with their advice. "Which side goes in first?" I asked. "Where do I fold the sleeves?" "How do we seal the package?" "Who am I?" "Where am I?" Who's disabled now?

In the panic of trying to keep up with the speed of my co-workers, I did just manage, here and there, to get a look at the artwork that was on the T- shirts. At first, the pictures appeared childlike. Yet, there was a resonance to them that I still remember today. I don't know how best to describe them other than to say that they had a soul and maturity; in other words, they were art. Pure. Beautiful. Art.

In the following pages we are reminded that it is innocence and humility coupled with the deep desire to express human thoughts and emotions that create any art of value. In *Disabled Fables* we are led into a world where the stories and the pictures create an experience very close to the dream of one's own childhood. I congratulate all the artists represented in this book, and I thank them for teaching me, among many other things, how to pack a T-shirt into a tight plastic wrapper, exhibiting the art without rumpling the sleeves.

— Sean Penn

Preface

This book was written and illustrated by people who have developmental disabilities. People with autism, Down syndrome, mental retardation, epilepsy, cerebral palsy, and other disabilities often have trouble telling stories in a linear way. They may start at the climax, jump to the end, and then go to the beginning. All the elements of the story are there, but they come out in disconnected fragments.

The artists who created *Disabled Fables* are all members of L.A. Goal, a non-profit agency that has been providing services for adults with developmental disabilities for 35 years. This book is the result of a project at L.A. Goal that invited twelve artists in the program to express themselves in a linear, "conventional" way by re-fashioning Aesop's fables in their own words and through their own artwork.

Each artist was asked to choose a fable that was meaningful to him or her – one that resonated with his or her life. The artists then reduced the fables into a series of images that showed the progression of the story. Each person decided how many pictures were needed to tell his or her story. Some chose to create many illustrations; others chose to use a single image. The artists then rewrote their fables in their own words and explained how the stories related to their lives. The artists worked on *Disabled Fables* for two years, and were paid for their work with funds raised by L.A. Goal.

The artists would like to acknowledge and thank L.A. Goal for recognizing and helping them to develop their abilities and strengths. In particular, they would like to thank Petite Konstantin, Susan Wilder, and Susan Baerwald who fostered and encouraged them in this endeavor. They also thank Mary Rojeski, Cindy Friedman, Margaret Goodenough, Glenn Ross, Werner Wolfen, Richard E. Posell, Jan Baum, Eve Elting, Betty Goldberg, Michelle Blackwell, Julie Popkin, Deborah Shine, and Carolyn Grifel.

The artists and L.A. Goal would like to thank the following people and organizations whose donations helped to make this book a reality: The Audrey and Sydney Irmas Charitable Foundation, Binney and Smith, Inc., Bernie Gainey at Promotions Distributor Services Corporation, Marjorie Kalins Taylor, Jeff Lamont and Dan Kavanaugh at Mirage Productions, and the Popkin Literary Agency.

THE FOX AND THE CAT

by Stephen Wise

Once upon a time there was a fox and a cat in the forest. They talked about clever ways to outsmart the huntsmen and the hounds. The fox, in a boasting mood, told the cat, "I have one hundred ideas in my bag of tricks about the best way to hide from our enemies." Then the cat said to the fox, "I have only one clever idea, but I will use it to protect myself."

When they heard the roaring sounds of the hounds, the huntsmen, and the galloping horses, the cat used his clever idea and ran up to a hidden branch in a high tree. He asked the fox what his plan was.

The fox, with his one hundred ideas, debated which one was the best. Meanwhile, the hounds and the huntsmen were getting closer and closer.

When the hounds and the huntsmen arrived, the fox realized he was in danger.

The fox saved himself by running out of the forest at the very last minute.

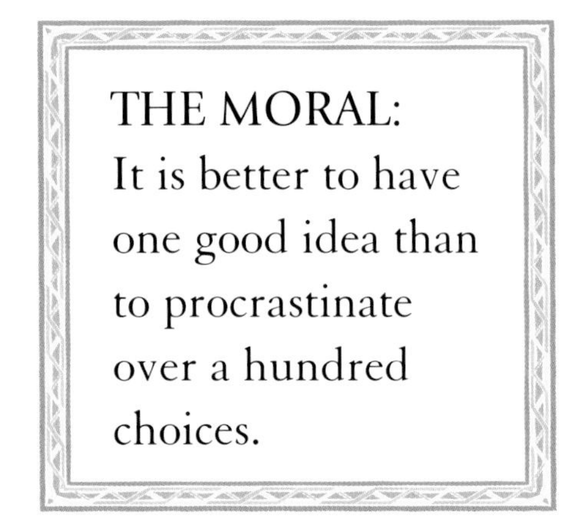

THE MORAL:
It is better to have one good idea than to procrastinate over a hundred choices.

WHAT THIS STORY MEANS TO ME

Like the fox, it is very hard for me to make the right decision because if I make a decision, I fear that it will be the wrong decision. There was a girl in my class that I wanted to get to know. I had a hundred ideas about how to start a conversation with her. I found out that she lived around the corner from the L.A. Goal office, but I couldn't decide which one of my hundred ideas to use. Because I hesitated, I didn't get to bring her in to the office and introduce her and show her my artwork like I wanted to.

My name is Stephen Wise. I'm a 24-year old adult with autism. I currently live in a two-bedroom apartment with a roommate. Last year, I graduated with honors from Santa Monica College with a B.A. in Music. I like doing artwork. With my drawings, I'm able to express myself to other people to show where I come from.

THE DEBONAIR CROW

by Robin Trocki

Once upon a time there was a debonair crow who was very thirsty. He flew all over New York City looking for a drink. He saw the Hudson River but he knew the water wasn't clean enough to drink.

Then he flew by a rooftop that had a pink table on it. On the table there was a pitcher with a very little bit of sparkling water left in it. It looked clean, and the crow just had to have some.

He tried to put his beak into the top of the pitcher to get a drink, but the opening was too small, and he couldn't reach the water.

But the crow kept trying. He looked around for a way to get to the clear sparkling water. Then he saw some colored stones on the roof.

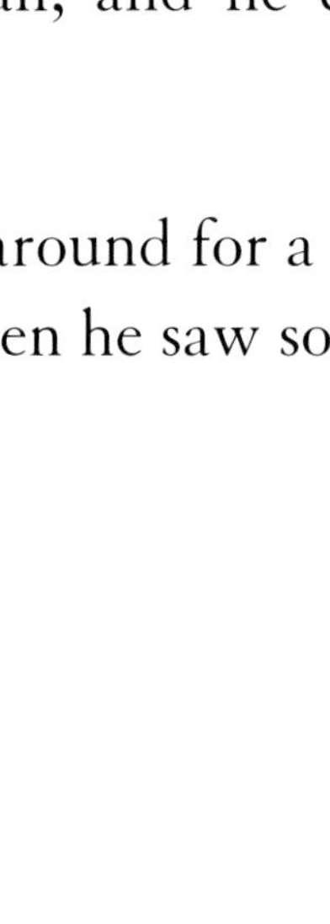

He took the stones one at a time and threw them into the pitcher. The water rose higher and higher.

Finally, when he had put enough pebbles in so he could reach the water, he got his drink. He was excited and felt proud because he hadn't given up and he had figured out how to get the water all by himself.

THE MORAL:
If you want something, don't give up. Try again, maybe in a different way.

WHAT THIS STORY MEANS TO ME

I was like the debonair crow at work. When I first started working, I thought the other people didn't like me because I was slow and different. But everyday I showed up and tried and tried to do my best. I worked hard to learn my job and asked for help when I needed it. Little by little, I learned my job and my coworkers became nice to me. I never gave up and I still have my job.

My name is Robin Trocki and I have Down syndrome. I'm not really happy about that, but I don't let it get in my way. I'm not different from anyone else once you get to know me. I live in my own apartment with a roommate. I work in the bakery department of a supermarket. I'm an athlete, an artist, a musician, a student, a good friend, and a happy person. I always try to be helpful. I have a good life and am very honored to be in this book.

THE MISERLY WOMAN

By Christine Monroe

A miserly woman dug a hole in her garden and buried her gold in it. Every week, she dug up the gold just to look at it and then put it back in the hole. One night, at the stroke of midnight, a robber came into the garden and stole the woman's gold.

The next day, the miserly woman came to dig up her gold once again, but it was gone. When she told everyone that her gold had been stolen, one of her neighbors asked, "Did you ever spend your money?"

"No, I just looked at it," the miserly woman answered.

So the neighbor said, "Then all you have to do is look at the hole. It's the same thing!"

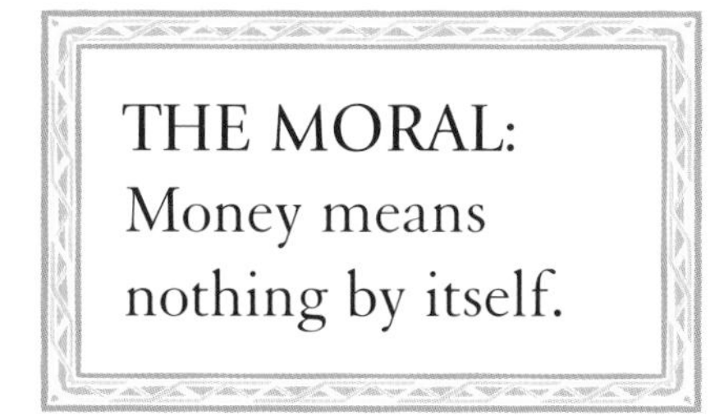

THE MORAL:
Money means nothing by itself.

WHAT THIS STORY MEANS TO ME

One day I went to buy groceries at the supermarket. I had a grocery list that my counselor had helped me write. I bought a lot of food all for myself. When I got home, I put the food away. I didn't want my sister to eat the food I had bought because I was afraid that if she ate it, there wouldn't be enough for me. I was selfish.

In fact, I bought more food than I really needed. Like the miserly woman, I kept it all for myself. Some of it got old and I had to throw it away. I could have shared some with my sister or my counselor, and it wouldn't have been wasted.

My name is Christine Monroe. I love to paint. I lived with my mother for 36 years. She took good care of me. My sister put me in the regional center on October 27, 1988, right after my mom was put in a retirement home. I got a job, worked hard, and was able to move out in 1993, and now I live with my sister. I work at Cedars Sinai Medical Center for the environmental service department, cleaning outside the plaza level. My work is very good and I am paid well.

THE CITY MOUSE AND THE COUNTRY MOUSE

by Shana Lavin

A city mouse went to visit his country cousin who welcomed him with open arms and offered him some simple, but delicious, country foods. The city mouse was quite shocked by the simplicity of his cousin's life. He told his cousin that if she came with him to the city, she'd see what real living was like and taste some really fancy foods.

Although she was very happy with her country life, what her cousin told her intrigued her. So the country mouse decided to visit her cousin's house in the city.

As promised, there were many good things to eat, and they feasted on a number of them.

At first, the country mouse was enjoying herself so much that she wondered how she could ever have lived otherwise. But just as she was thinking that, some loud, barking dogs rushed into the room, and she was terribly frightened.

The country mouse fled from the house as fast as she could, afraid for her life. She decided that she would rather live a peaceful, simple country life than face the dangers of the big city.

THE MORAL: It's better to live in peace than in pieces.

WHAT THIS STORY MEANS TO ME:

I'm a city girl, but I always dreamed of living in the country. Once I went to visit some friends in the country, and I loved it. There were simple, fresh-grown foods, lots of plants, rivers and trees, clean air. . . everything that couldn't be found in the city. I wanted to live there so badly; I started talking to my friends to see if I could find a job in the country so I could move there.

I soon discovered that there were only two industries there–farming and logging–neither of which I could do, for I knew very little about them. I am qualified to work as an emergency medical technician, not as a farmer or logger. What's more, the closest hospital that I could either work at or go to was forty miles away, and I can't drive.

As much as I would have liked to live in the country, I cannot be without a job or a nearby hospital so I must remain a city girl for now. I must be content with what I have, instead of trying to live out a dream.

My name is Shana Lavin, and I am a 42-year-old college student, majoring in chemical technology. I am currently in my second semester of studies and I am taking physics, music, and body conditioning. I have been an emergency medical technician for the past four years. I was born and raised in Los Angeles, and I belong to Chaverim and L.A. Goal. I like writing poetry and crocheting.

THE JAY AND THE PEACOCK

by Helen Pacheco

One spring day, a jay bird flew into the woods, looking for something to do. There he spied some beautiful peacock feathers on the ground. He thought that he would look pretty if he had colorful feathers, so he flew down and tied the feathers to his tail.

Then he paraded himself in front of the peacocks, showing off all his new feathers.

When the peacocks saw him, they laughed at him and plucked the feathers off, while his brothers mocked him for not being himself.

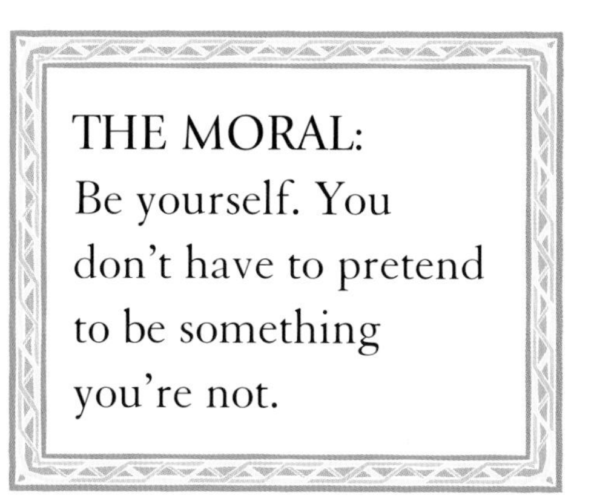

THE MORAL:
Be yourself. You don't have to pretend to be something you're not.

WHAT THIS STORY MEANS TO ME:

I have always been overweight and have tried many diets. My friends and family have always teased me about my weight. Once I got down to 109 pounds and I felt great about myself. Then I went overseas. I came back and I started to gain weight again. I realize that I have to live with myself whether I am fat or not. Nowadays, my friends and family understand that, and they don't tease me as much. I'm still fat and still dieting, but I feel O.K. about myself.

My name is Helen Pacheco. I'm 35 years old. I have been painting for a long time and I enjoy it. I like bright colors, especially blue. I've been working downtown for thirteen years. I'm a clerk at Legal Service Industries. I enjoy reading, writing, singing, and drama, as well as art class.

THE SHEPHERD BOY

by Todd Rubien

Once upon a time, in a faraway village, there was a shepherd boy who lived a very lonely life. Day after day, hour after hour, he sat on a mountaintop, guarding his flock of sheep against an attack by wolves.

The shepherd boy grew so tired of being alone that he devised a plan he felt sure would bring people to talk to him. He stood on the very top of the hill, and cried out, "Wolf! Wolf!" at the top of his voice.

Immediately, everyone in town came running to the hilltop. Finding no wolf, the astonished people questioned the boy. Realizing they had been fooled, the crowd sharply admonished the lad and went back to town.

Despite the reprimand, the next day when he was feeling lonely, the boy again let out another false cry of "Wolf! Wolf!" Once again the townspeople came running. This time they were even angrier at being fooled. They gave the lad an even stronger admonishment.

The next morning, the boy spotted a real wolf and sounded a real alarm by crying, "Wolf! Wolf!"

This time, however, the townspeople decided the boy was pretending again, and they did not respond. The wolf got away with two of the sheep, and the boy learned a valuable lesson.

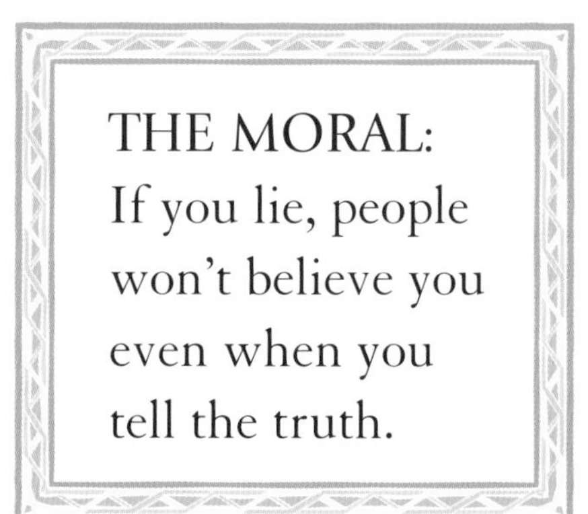

THE MORAL:
If you lie, people won't believe you even when you tell the truth.

WHAT THIS STORY MEANS TO ME

The story of the *The Shepherd Boy* appeals to me because it deals with loneliness. It is especially poignant for me because it represents the feelings of utter frustration I felt as a child, growing up friendless and unwanted because I was different and acted differently than the other students in school.

In this story, the boy learns that creating a false emergency is the wrong way to combat loneliness. Sharing feelings and talking about emotions in a straight-forward way is a good base for beginning a friendship.

It took me years of heartbreak and pain before I learned to accept this idea. Once I learned to accept people in my life as friends instead of enemies, a new light dawned. It was as if I had been born into the world again. When we allow the light of friendship into our lives, the glow passes on to everyone who crosses our paths.

My name is Todd Rubien. I'm 43 years old. I attended West L.A. Junior College where I received my B.A. in Fine Arts as a music major. I enjoy classical music, movies, and being with my friends at L.A. Goal, where I've been a member for 16 years. My art background started with Susan Wilder, the woman who runs the art program at L.A. Goal. I had no art training before that. From the first class, she helped me realize that we all have potential, no matter what our disabilities. From this I have learned that, no matter what our disabilities are, we still have value to society.

THE TWO GOATS

By Robert Schwartz

One day, two proud goats coming from different directions were determined to cross a narrow bridge. But there was one problem–each goat felt that it was his turn to go first across the bridge.

They battled it out head to head because neither would back up. They tried to push past each other. But with each goat pushing and shoving against the other, they both fell off the narrow bridge into the rough waters below.

THE MORAL: We should all take turns and cooperate with each other to get what we want.

WHAT THIS STORY MEANS TO ME

One day after camp, my friend Charlie and forty-nine other campers were waiting in line for the bus to go home. Charlie liked to be first in line so he could sit in the front row of the bus. But another guy also wanted to go on first, so there was a big problem. Both Charlie and the other guy were really aggravated. Charlie was already in line first, but the other guy also wanted to sit in the front seat and knew he wouldn't have a chance if he wasn't first in line.

He started to push and shove Charlie, and there was fighting, hitting, and kicking and they both got hurt. What they didn't notice was that there were front seats on both sides of the bus, so both of them could have had what they wanted without fighting about it. If they had taken turns and cooperated with each other, they both would have gotten what they wanted.

I'm Robert E. Schwartz, and I'm 36 years old. I live on my own and enjoy it. I have a girlfriend. I work at Bear Stearns as an operator, and I also do some filing and organizing. I enjoy listening to music and drawing. This fable project took a lot of thinking and figuring out. Writing a story takes a lot of concentration and a lot of patience.

THE TORTOISE AND THE HARE

by Elizabeth Cooper

The hare was teasing the tortoise because he was so slow. The tortoise was ashamed and embarrassed by the hare's teasing, but he didn't run away from his troubles. He stood up for himself and said to the hare, "This is the way I'm made."

The hare laughed at the tortoise and said, "I bet I could beat you in a race."

The tortoise agreed to the race, thinking to himself, "I'll do the best I can." He didn't worry about winning or losing. The hare laughed and went to his friend the fox to organize the race. He invited the other forest animals to watch so they could have a good laugh.

The tortoise stood at the starting line, knowing he was sure to lose. But he felt proud to be getting so much attention. Soon the race began.

As usual, the hare was a show-off while the tortoise went at his own pace. The forest animals were sure the hare was going to win.

Because the tortoise was taking a long time, and it was a beautiful sunny day, and everyone had plenty to eat and drink, some of the forest animals lost interest and fell asleep. The hare was so far ahead he decided to take a nap, too.

The tortoise saw the hare sleeping, but he didn't stop. He passed the sleeping hare and headed to the finish line.

The tortoise won! The forest animals were astonished and thrilled.

THE MORAL: If you keep trying, even if you're not the fastest or the strongest, you can still win.

WHAT THIS STORY MEANS TO ME

One day, I was trying to tell something to a staff person at City Community Services. I had thought of what I was going to say beforehand, but when I started to talk, I had a little difficulty getting my thoughts out.

The woman asked me to talk faster. I think she was a little impatient. I felt a little bad inside, and mad, and then I got over it. I would like to have my thoughts come out smoother. I am practicing every day. I can see my words rushing around in my head, but I struggle and I can't always get them out. I feel like my throat is hoarse. I take slow breaths, in and out, and then a lot of the time, I can get my thoughts out. I'm doing much better.

I know that people are impatient because they don't know what I'm going to say. I know they are in a rush and that is frustrating for me, but I am trying my best. I will get my thoughts out eventually. I try to remember that I'm like the tortoise. I'll get there in the end.

My name is Elisabeth Cooper. I have four older brothers. I was born in Paris, France. I lived in Brooklyn Heights, New York, and then Los Angeles for twelve years. Then I lived in Santa Barbara and drove down to L.A. Goal once a week with my mother. I now live in a communal village and work on a farm.

THE CRANE

by Lisa Yalowitz

A crane went out one day to get some fish for her meal. This crane was very picky. She wanted the most perfect fish, so she searched and searched.

A lot of fish went by but none of them looked good enough. It got to be late, and the crane could not see well any more. Because she was so picky, she didn't get any dinner at all.

THE MORAL:
You can end up with nothing when everything has to be perfect. Nothing is ever perfect.

WHAT THIS STORY MEANS TO ME

When I first started painting, I did not like anything that I painted because some of the things were too messy. I felt that everything had to be neat and perfect. I didn't think my work was good enough, so I wouldn't save it. Now I regret throwing away some of my artwork because I probably would be more accepting of it now.

My name is Lisa Yalowitz. I'm legally blind in one eye. But that has not stopped me from accomplishing things, or from doing normal everyday tasks that need to be done, or from doing what I enjoy, such as my artwork, reading, and cooking. Although I may need help at times, I am comfortable asking for it. I have been a member of L.A. Goal since 1995.

THE DOG AND HIS SHADOW

Lisa Finkelor

One day, a reverse dalmatian dug up a rather meaty bone. He had no doggy bag so he decided to carry it home in his mouth.

On his way home, he had to cross a bridge over a lake. As the dalmatian started to cross the bridge, he saw another dog reflected on the surface of the lake. His bone looked larger. The dalmation was so greedy that he wanted that bone, too.

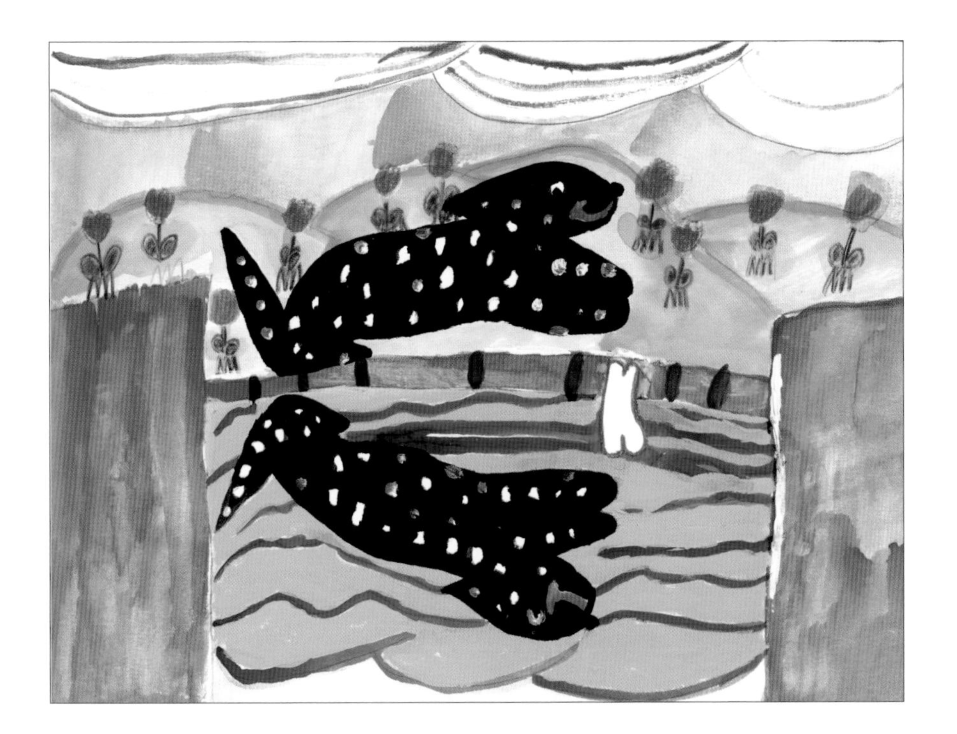

As he reached for the other dog's bone, the dalmation let go of the bone he had in his mouth. It fell into the lake and was lost forever. The dalmatian was surprised and then sad. He went home with no dinner at all.

THE MORAL: Don't be greedy. If you want what others have, you might lose what you already have yourself.

WHAT THIS STORY MEANS TO ME

Sometimes on holidays or my birthday, I keep asking for more and more things. I ask for what I want, or I make lists, but I would really be happy with just a couple of things. When I keep asking for a lot of things, I am being greedy. And if I am greedy, I lose out on what I already have. I either get what I want or I don't, and it should be O.K. either way.

My name is Lisa Caren Finkelor and I am 33 years old. I live with my friends at Eras House II. Sometimes I visit the house where I lived with my parents when I was a baby. I like swimming, reading, writing, math, art, drawing, painting, and playing games.

THE BEAR AND THE BEES

by Joe Mills

Once there was a big brown bear who was searching for berries in the woods when he noticed a hollow log. The bear went toward the log and was sniffing it cautiously when a bee spotted him. The bee quickly flew over to the bear and stung him on the nose.

This made the bear so mad that he started to tear the log apart, causing all the bees to come out and sting him. In a panic, the bear ran and dove into a nearby pond, where he stayed until the bees flew away.

THE MORAL:
Don't be a fool by letting your anger take over your good judgement.

WHAT THIS STORY MEANS TO ME:

I get angry at work when the other employees joke about me. One employee made a joke by telling me to mop the ceilings. This joke got me really upset so I told him to do his work while I did mine. I controlled my anger by not raising my voice because I could have lost my job. Losing my job would have been worse than getting stung like the bear.

My name is Joe Mills. I'm 42 and I have autism. Even though I'm autistic, I have a very good memory. I've been an L.A. Goal member for 21 years and I like to paint with acrylic. I also have a number of other interests. I like entertaining kids by doing a clown act and by making animals out of balloons. I like going to Las Vegas. For 9 years I have had a job at Vons Market working as a courtesy clerk.

THE DOVE AND THE ANT

by Helen Pacheco

A very thirsty ant was about to drink from a river when a strong wind blew the ant into the water.

A dove, flying above, saw the ant in distress and dropped a fallen branch into the river to help the ant. The ant climbed on to the branch and out of the river–safe at last!

Later that day, a bird catcher spied the beautiful dove and laid his trap. The ant happened to see the man hiding in a bushy tree, watching the dove.

Just as the dove flew up, the man tried to catch her in his net. But the ant bit the man's toe. He was so startled that he dropped the net, and the dove flew away safely.

THE MORAL: If you do something nice for someone, someone might do something nice for you.

WHAT THIS STORY MEANS TO ME

I was walking to my mom's place one day after art class. I had a headache and I was feeling really tired. I had half a mile to go and was wondering if I could make it. Just then a friend drove by. I was surprised to see her and relieved when she stopped and offered to give me a lift. I got into the car and I was grateful for the ride. I thanked her and promised I'd help her out sometime if I could.

The following week, my friend had a doctor's appointment and had to miss work, so I did her job of addressing and sealing envelopes. I was glad to help her because she had helped me. Thank you, Jeanette. I really appreciated your help. Now, at my own job, I'm doing all the mail, so my good deed helped me out in return!

THE FOX AND THE GRAPES

by Stephen Wise

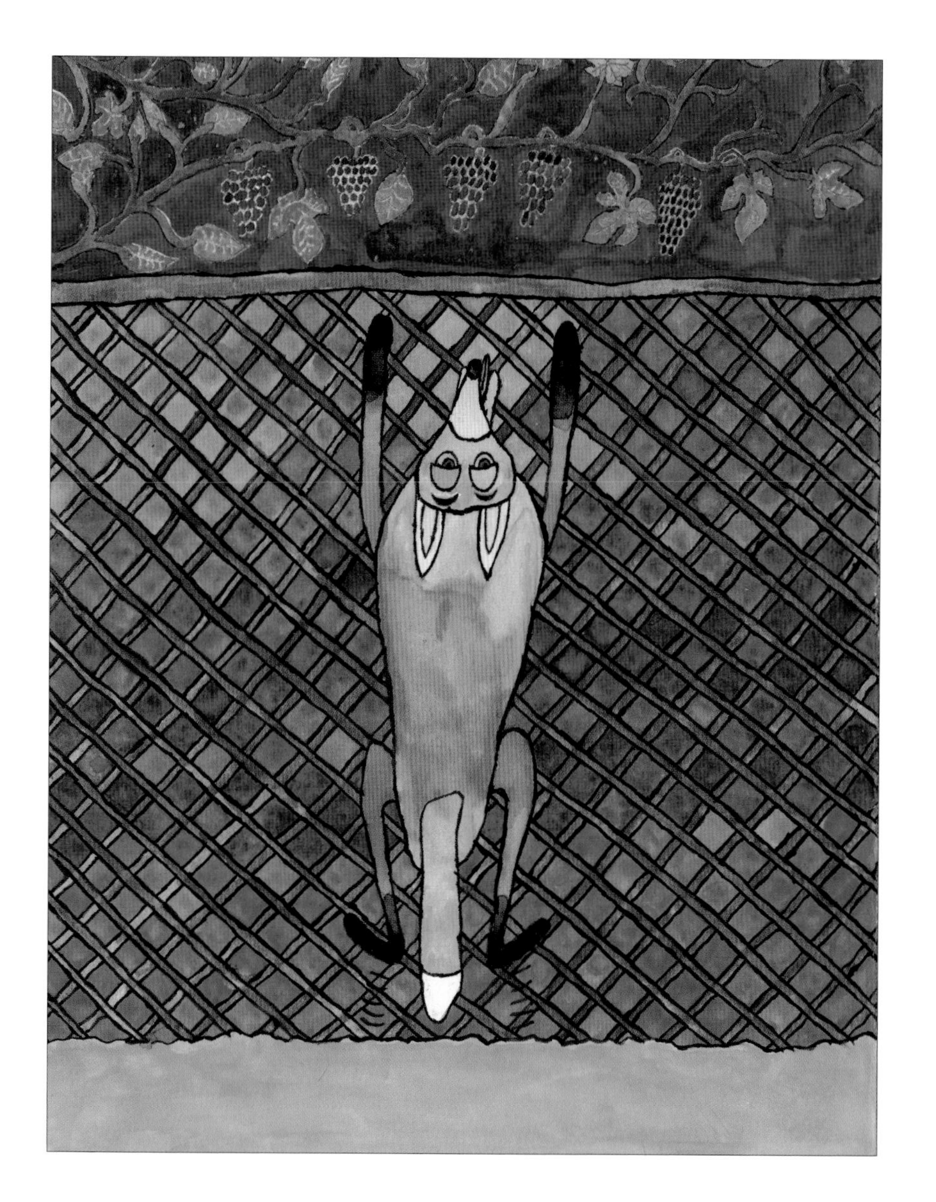

One hot summer day, a fox took a walk through an orchard and saw some grapes high up on a branch. Since he was hungry, he decided to try to get some of them.

The fox stepped back a little, ran toward the grape vine, and jumped up. Even though he repeated this process over and over again, he couldn't reach the grapes. He never managed to jump high enough to reach them.

Finally, the fox gave up and walked away. As he was leaving, he looked back at the grapes and decided that they were probably sour anyway, and that he didn't really want them after all.

THE MORAL: If you can't have what you really want, it's better to move on and forget about it.

WHAT THIS STORY MEANS TO ME

I enrolled in a string-instrument class that required I have either a bass, cello, viola, or violin. I decided that I wanted a violin, but I couldn't afford to buy one. The teacher arranged for me to rent one for the semester. When the semester ended, I had to return the violin to my teacher.

I made a friend in that class, which was not easy for me. Her husband has a violin, and she let me borrow it for a while. I know that I'll have to give it back soon, and I'll have to settle for playing music on my electric keyboard instead of the violin. I could pretend that I didn't like the violin class, like the fox did with the grapes, even though I really did like it.

THE LION AND THE MOUSE

by Elaine Hartman

A lion was sleeping when a mouse ran over to him. The lion woke up and caught the mouse in his large paw and wanted to eat him. The mouse pleaded for his life, "Please don't eat me, lion. Our paths might cross again, and if you spare my life, I could do you a favor someday."

"I'm the king," the lion thought. "What could this little guy do for me?" But since the lion wasn't hungry anyway, he decided to let the mouse go.

A couple of months later, the lion found himself in serious trouble. Some hunters had caught him and tied him down. The lion was wondering how he was going to get out of the situation when he heard a tiny whisper. It was the mouse. He had forgotten all about him.

"It looks like you need some help," the mouse said.

"Well, what can *you* do about it?" roared the lion.

The mouse didn't say anything but started gnawing on the ropes that held the lion down. After a few hours, he had completely chewed through them, and the lion was free.

"Thank you. You saved my life," said the lion. "I never thought a little mouse could save the king of the jungle."

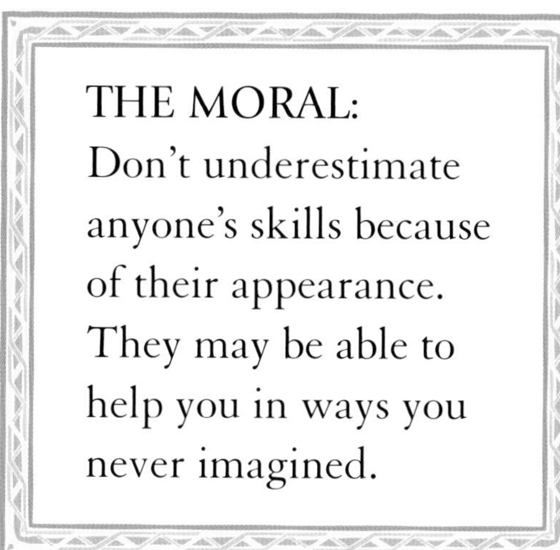

THE MORAL:
Don't underestimate anyone's skills because of their appearance. They may be able to help you in ways you never imagined.

WHAT THIS STORY MEANS TO ME

I see a therapist who has a hearing disability. Because of her disability, I didn't know if she would be able to help me. But after I had worked with her for a while, I realized that she was able to relate to me because of her disability and help me with my own, maybe even more than a therapist who doesn't have a disability.

Some people judge me first by my disability instead of trying to understand who I am. That is hurtful. I wish that people would take the time to get to know me before they judge me.

My name is Elaine Hartman. I have studied Kandinsky and Klee, and I'm interested in all styles of art. One of my art pieces was picked to be in an art show and won an honorable mention. I felt very good about receiving that honor. I like art because its value is in the eye of the beholder.

About L.A. Goal

L.A. Goal is a non-profit organization based in Culver City, California. It was founded in 1969 to serve adults with developmental disabilities such as autism, mental retardation, Down syndrome, learning disabilities, and neurological problems, including epilepsy and cerebral palsy. Its mission is to empower each member to reach his or her fullest potential, and to ensure that all members receive the practical training and emotional support they need. L.A. Goal members are encouraged to recognize and utilize their personal abilities and strengths, allowing them to take risks and explore new ways of learning. This raises their self-esteem and increases their independence. L.A. Goal's programs have been designed around this philosophy; they include visual arts, sewing, music, drama, clinical services, counseling, vocational training, physical fitness, and training in social skills and interactions. Practical and emotional support is available for members' families.

In 1995, L.A. Goal launched Inside Out Productions, a non-profit business venture that employs members and sells the artwork they produce. Their art has been displayed and sold in numerous boutiques, galleries, and museums.